THE FIRST RED MAPLE LEAF

LUDMILA ZEMAN

TUNDRA BOOKS

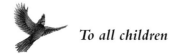 *To all children*

Copyright © 1997 Ludmila Zeman
First Paperback Edition, 1997

Published in Canada by Tundra Books, *McClelland & Stewart Young Readers*,
481 University Avenue, Toronto, Ontario M5G 2E9

Published in the United States by Tundra Books of Northern New York,
P.O. Box 1030, Plattsburgh, New York 12901

Library of Congress Catalog Number: 96-60350

Canadian Cataloguing in Publication Data

Zeman, Ludmila
  The first red maple leaf

ISBN 0-88776-372-3 (bound)   ISBN 0-88776-419-3 (pbk.)

1. Maple leaf (Emblem) – Juvenile literature. I. Title.

CR212.Z45 1997   j929.9'0971   C96-900251-3

We acknowledge the support of the Canada Council for the Arts for our publishing program.

Design: Sari Ginsberg

Printed and bound in Canada

1 2 3 4 5 6   02 01 00 99 98 97

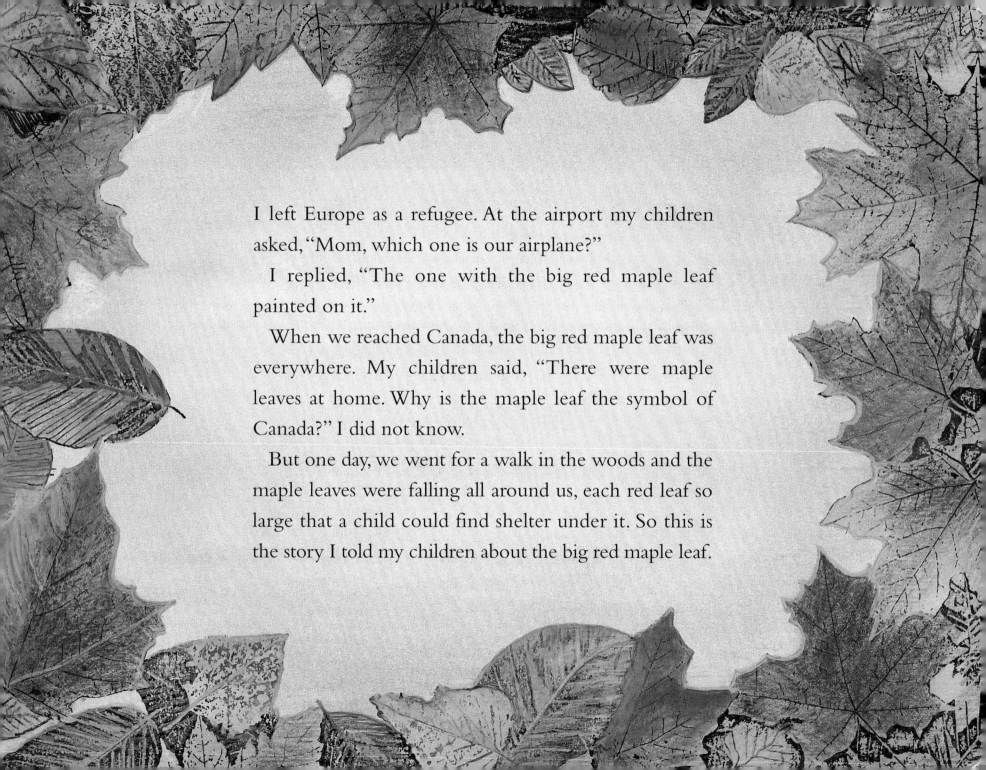

I left Europe as a refugee. At the airport my children asked, "Mom, which one is our airplane?"

I replied, "The one with the big red maple leaf painted on it."

When we reached Canada, the big red maple leaf was everywhere. My children said, "There were maple leaves at home. Why is the maple leaf the symbol of Canada?" I did not know.

But one day, we went for a walk in the woods and the maple leaves were falling all around us, each red leaf so large that a child could find shelter under it. So this is the story I told my children about the big red maple leaf.

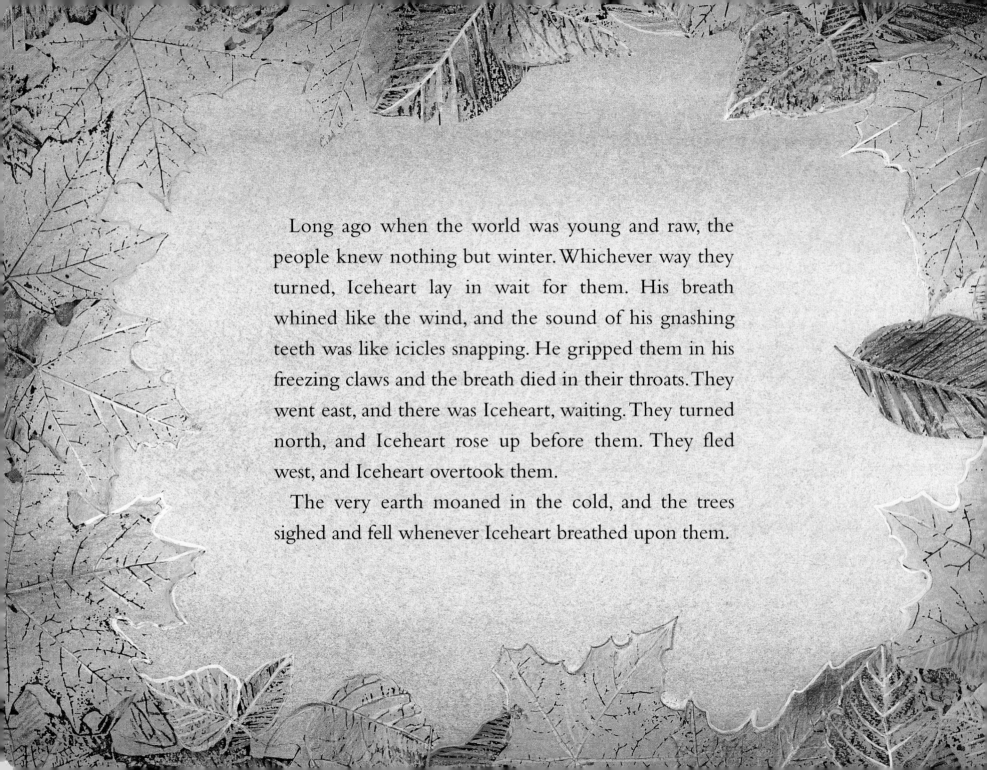

Long ago when the world was young and raw, the people knew nothing but winter. Whichever way they turned, Iceheart lay in wait for them. His breath whined like the wind, and the sound of his gnashing teeth was like icicles snapping. He gripped them in his freezing claws and the breath died in their throats. They went east, and there was Iceheart, waiting. They turned north, and Iceheart rose up before them. They fled west, and Iceheart overtook them.

The very earth moaned in the cold, and the trees sighed and fell whenever Iceheart breathed upon them.

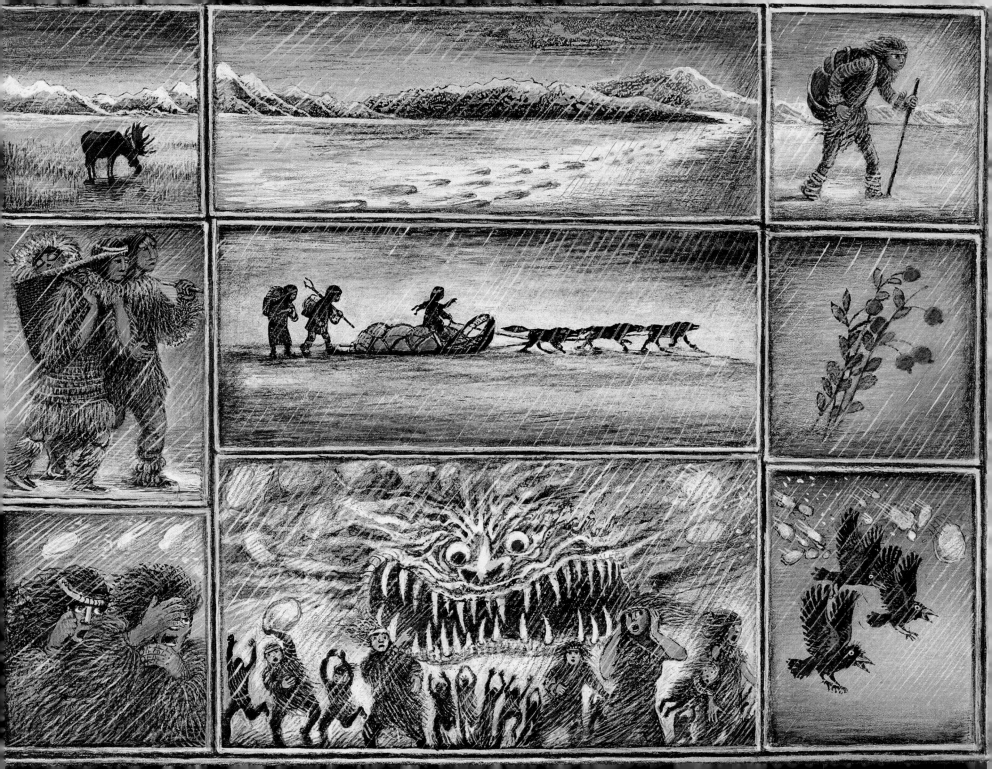

As one tree dropped frozen and dead in the snow, Branta the goose lay trapped beneath it. A child of the people ran to gather up the goose thinking, 'Here is food', but Branta cried, "Spare my life and I will lead you to safety." Then the boy set the goose free. Iceheart watched with angry eyes.

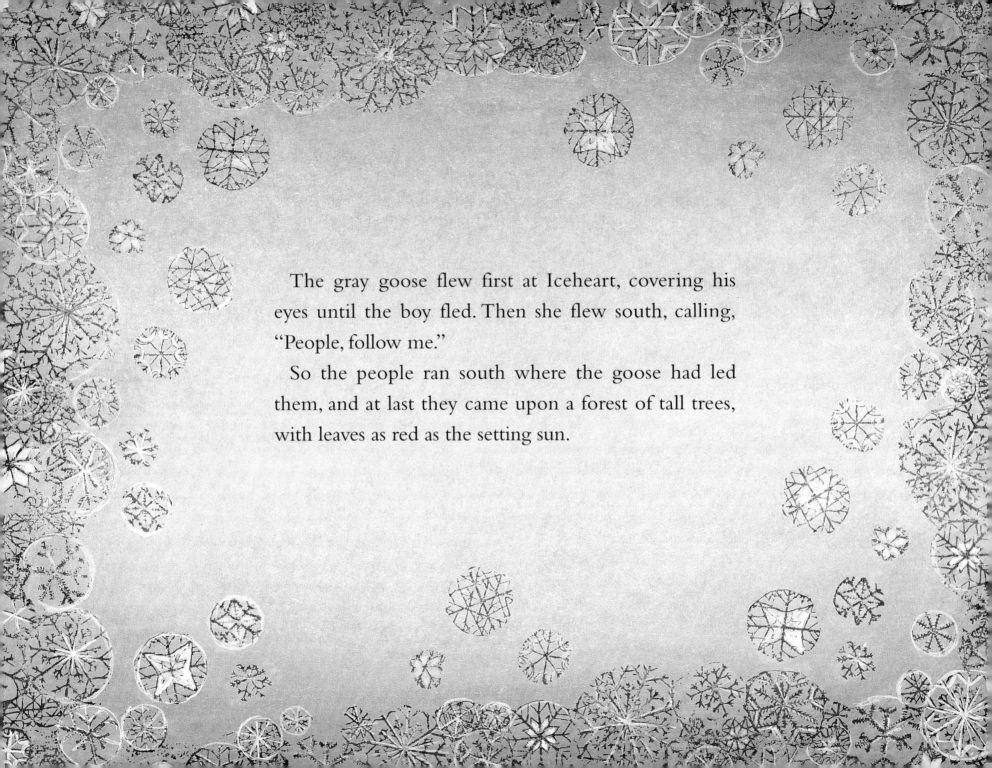

The gray goose flew first at Iceheart, covering his eyes until the boy fled. Then she flew south, calling, "People, follow me."

So the people ran south where the goose had led them, and at last they came upon a forest of tall trees, with leaves as red as the setting sun.

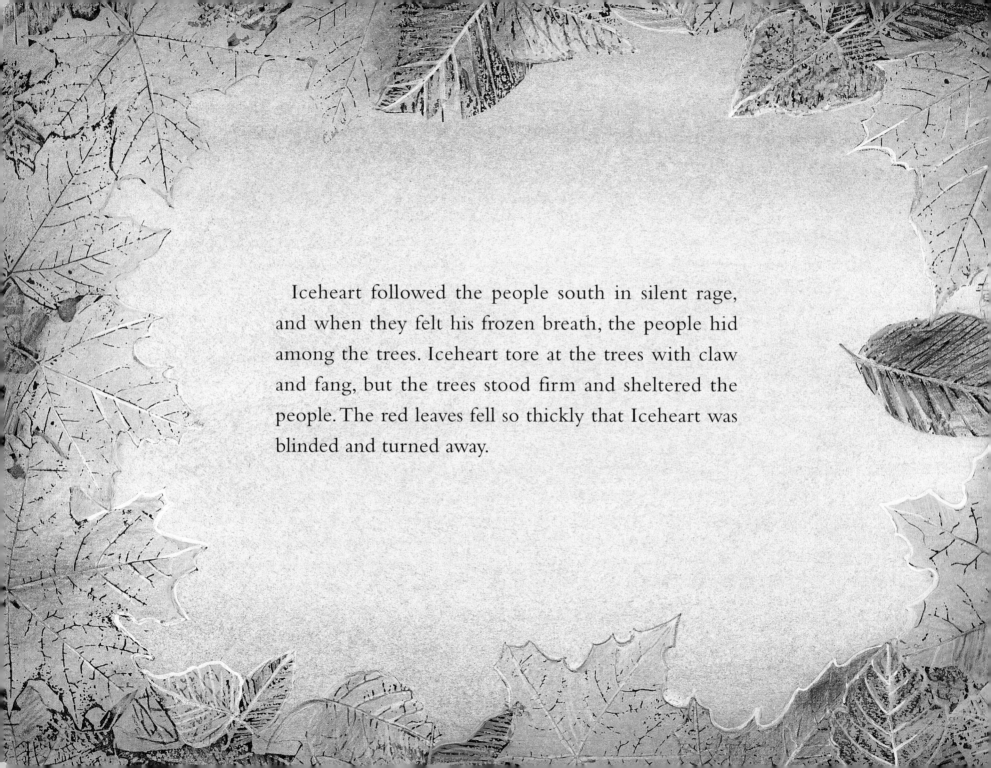

Iceheart followed the people south in silent rage, and when they felt his frozen breath, the people hid among the trees. Iceheart tore at the trees with claw and fang, but the trees stood firm and sheltered the people. The red leaves fell so thickly that Iceheart was blinded and turned away.

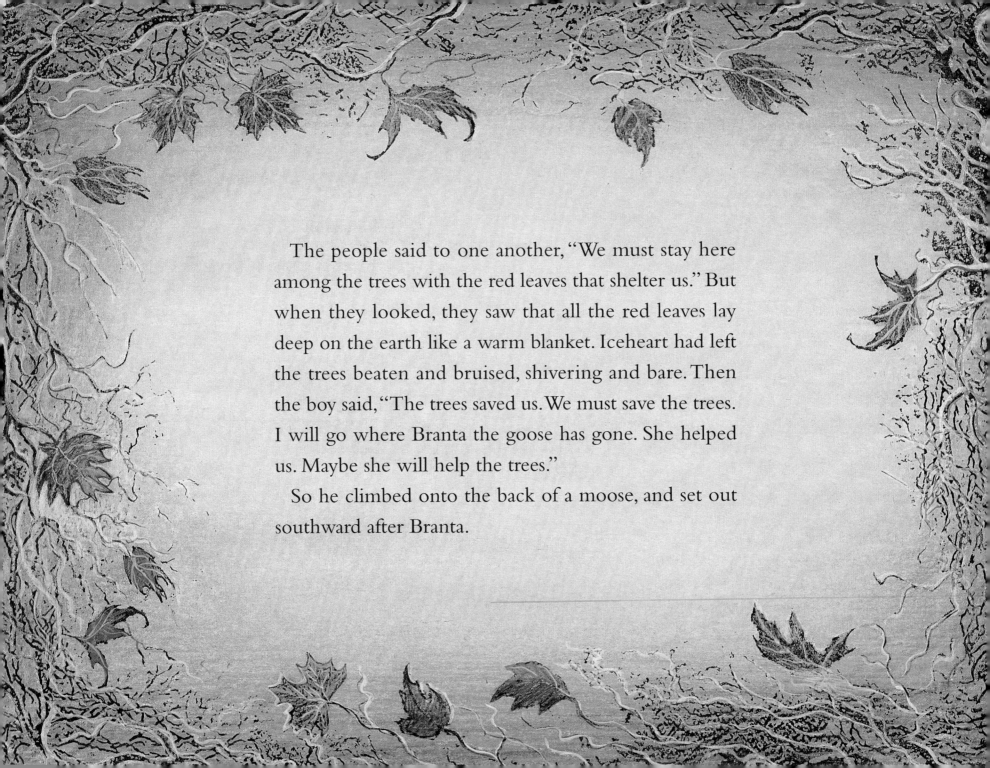

The people said to one another, "We must stay here among the trees with the red leaves that shelter us." But when they looked, they saw that all the red leaves lay deep on the earth like a warm blanket. Iceheart had left the trees beaten and bruised, shivering and bare. Then the boy said, "The trees saved us. We must save the trees. I will go where Branta the goose has gone. She helped us. Maybe she will help the trees."

So he climbed onto the back of a moose, and set out southward after Branta.

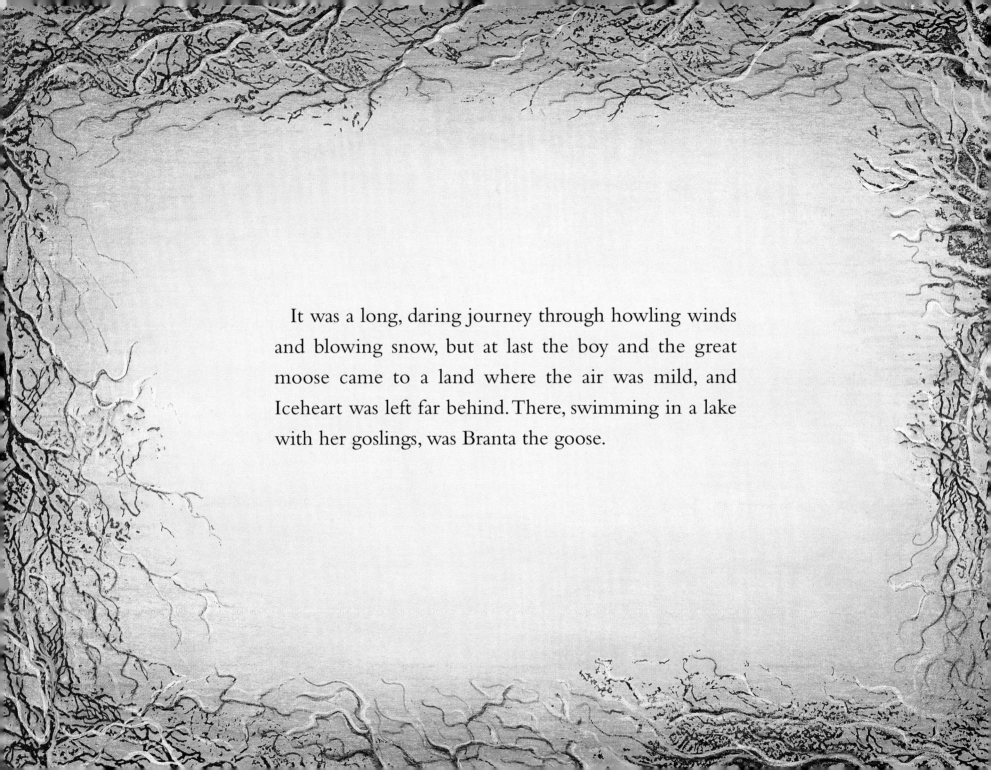

It was a long, daring journey through howling winds and blowing snow, but at last the boy and the great moose came to a land where the air was mild, and Iceheart was left far behind. There, swimming in a lake with her goslings, was Branta the goose.

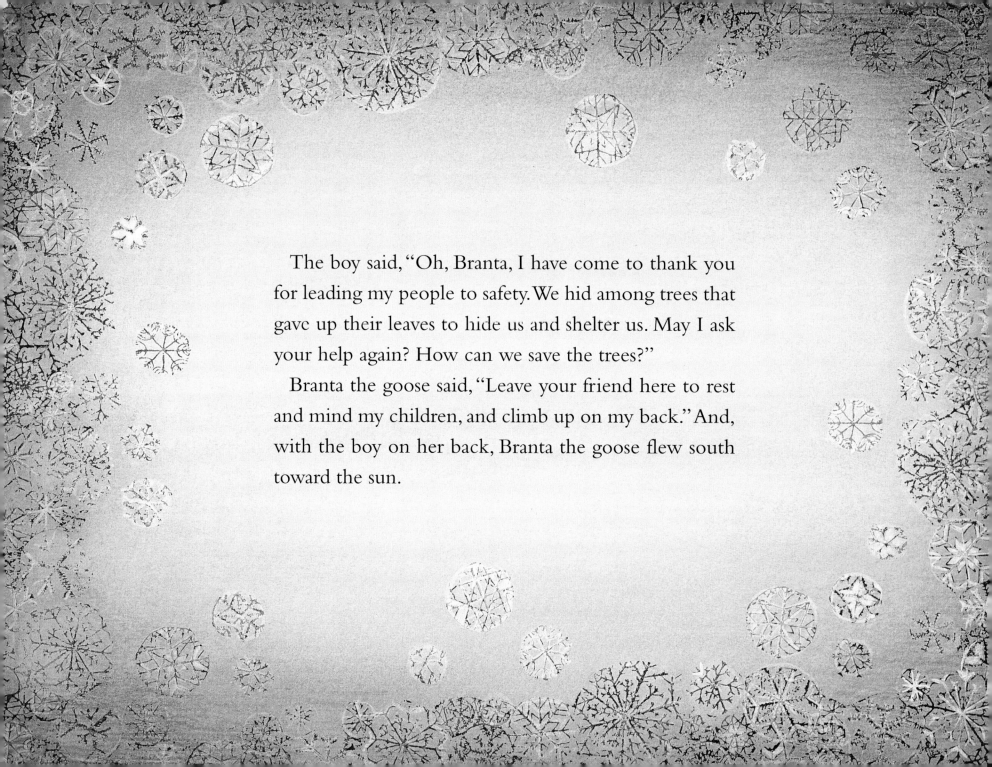

The boy said, "Oh, Branta, I have come to thank you for leading my people to safety. We hid among trees that gave up their leaves to hide us and shelter us. May I ask your help again? How can we save the trees?"

Branta the goose said, "Leave your friend here to rest and mind my children, and climb up on my back." And, with the boy on her back, Branta the goose flew south toward the sun.

At last they came to a land more beautiful and full of color than the boy had ever seen, a land where the trees were always green and so filled with bright, singing birds that the boy could not tell birds from leaves. Branta the goose called the birds to her and told them of the trees in the north that had lost their leaves.

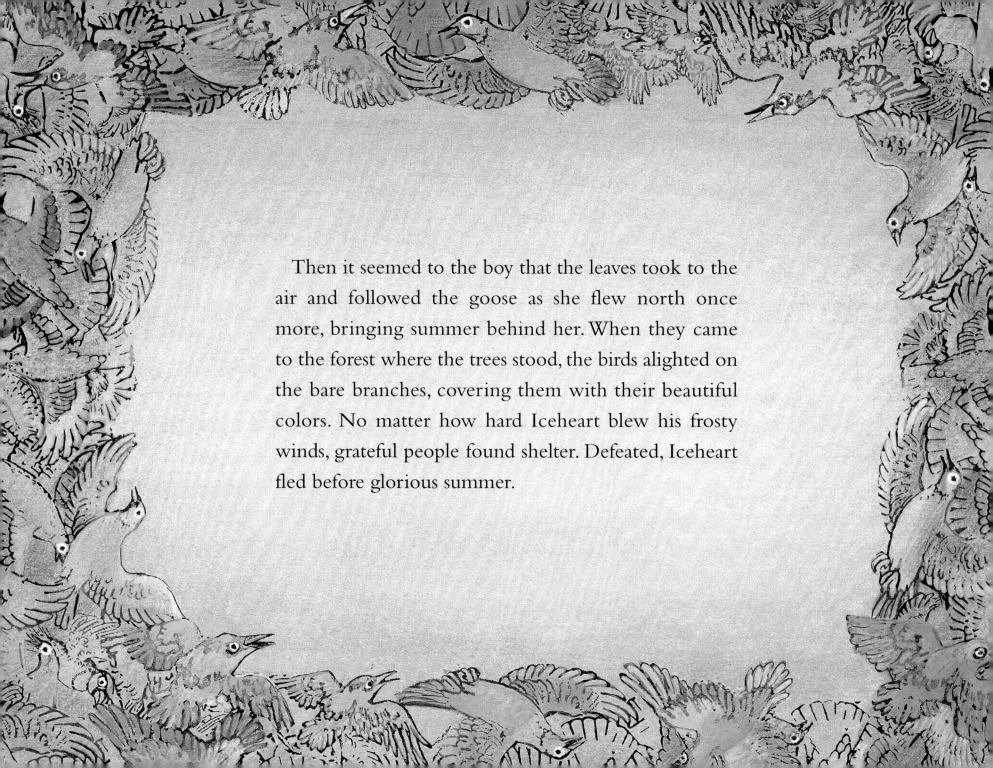

Then it seemed to the boy that the leaves took to the air and followed the goose as she flew north once more, bringing summer behind her. When they came to the forest where the trees stood, the birds alighted on the bare branches, covering them with their beautiful colors. No matter how hard Iceheart blew his frosty winds, grateful people found shelter. Defeated, Iceheart fled before glorious summer.

"But we cannot stay here always," said Branta the goose. "In winter we must fly south once more, but never fear, for all time winter and summer will take turns and the leaves will always come again."

Whatever the season, the red maple leaf shelters my new country. For me, it represents the sense of safety I felt when I first came here with my family.